First published 1993
by Walker Books Ltd
87 Vauxhall Walk, London SE11 5HJ

This edition published 2007

8 10 9 7

Printed in China

British Library Cataloguing in Publication Data:
a catalogue record for this book
is available from the British Library

ISBN 978-1-4063-1076-4

www.walker.co.uk

Washing Line

Jez Alborough

WALKER BOOKS
AND SUBSIDIARIES
LONDON • BOSTON • SYDNEY • AUCKLAND

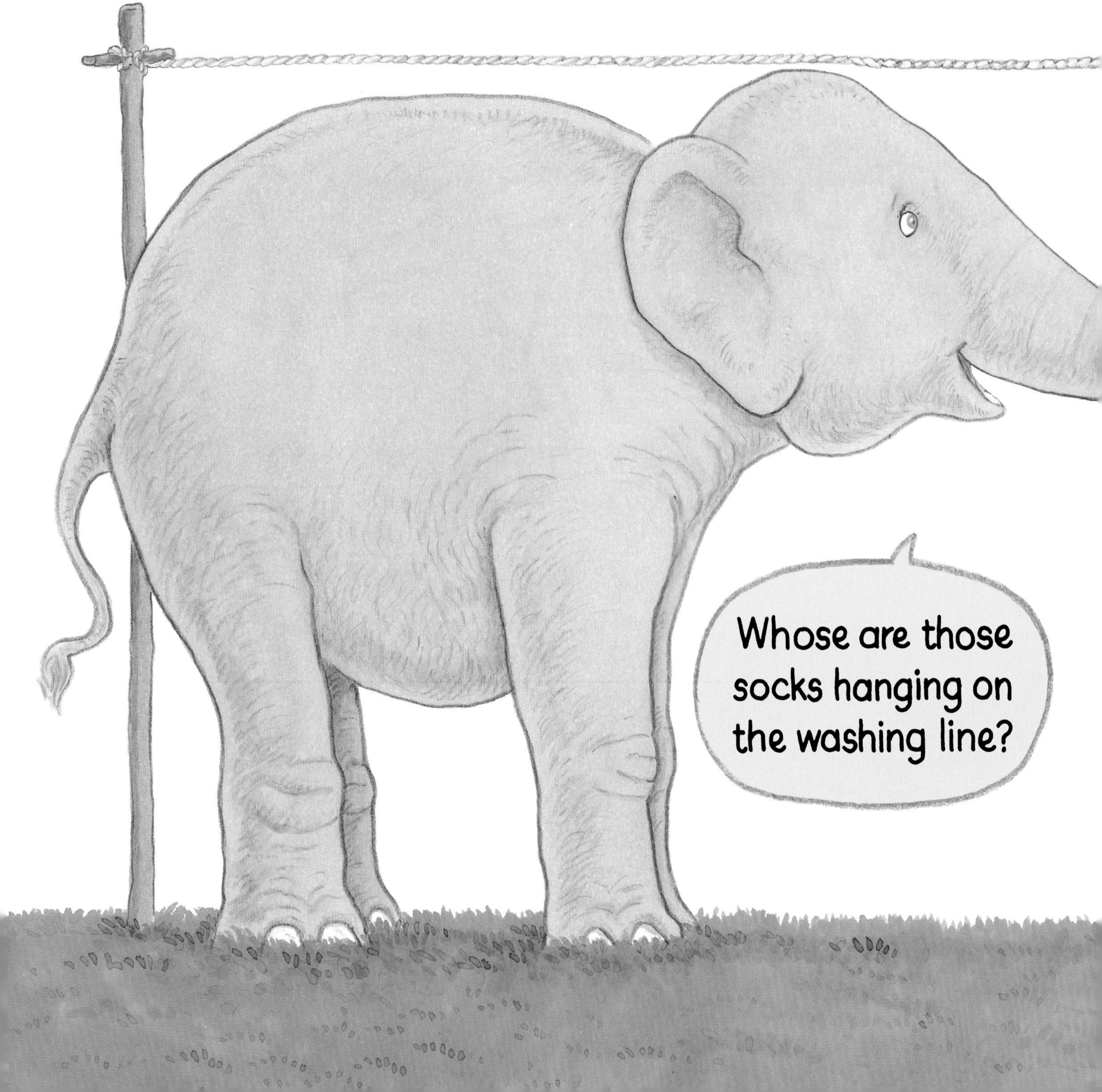
Whose are those socks hanging on the washing line?

asked the elephant.

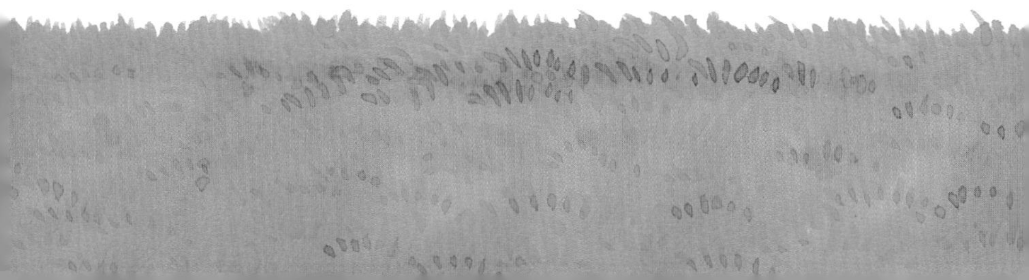

said the flamingo.

Whose is that jumper hanging on the washing line?

asked the elephant
and the flamingo.

It's mine

grunted the
orang-utan.

Whose is that dress hanging on the washing line?

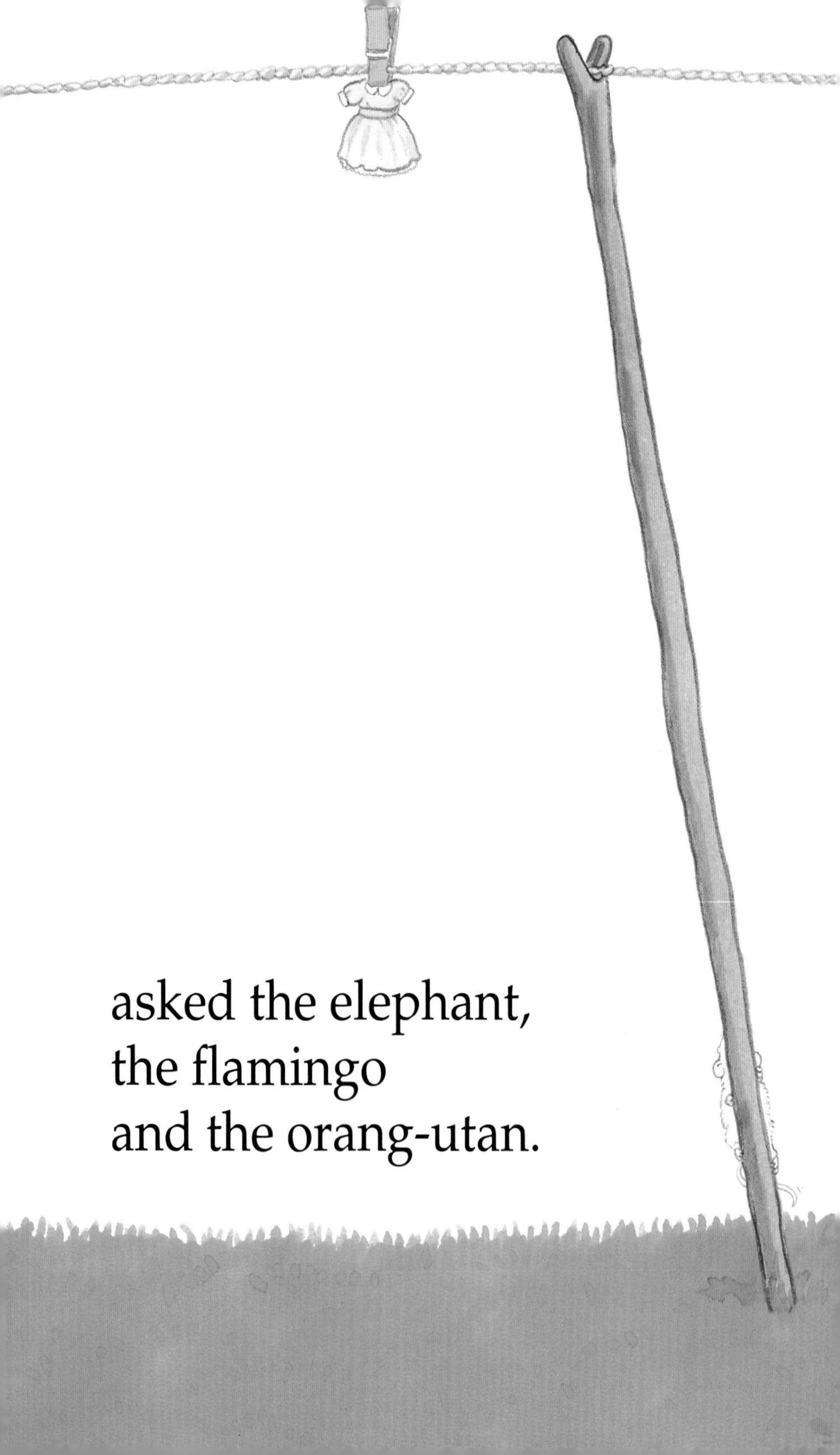

asked the elephant,
the flamingo
and the orang-utan.

said the mouse.

Whose is that scarf hanging on the washing line?

Whose are those underpants hanging on the washing line?

said the giraffe.

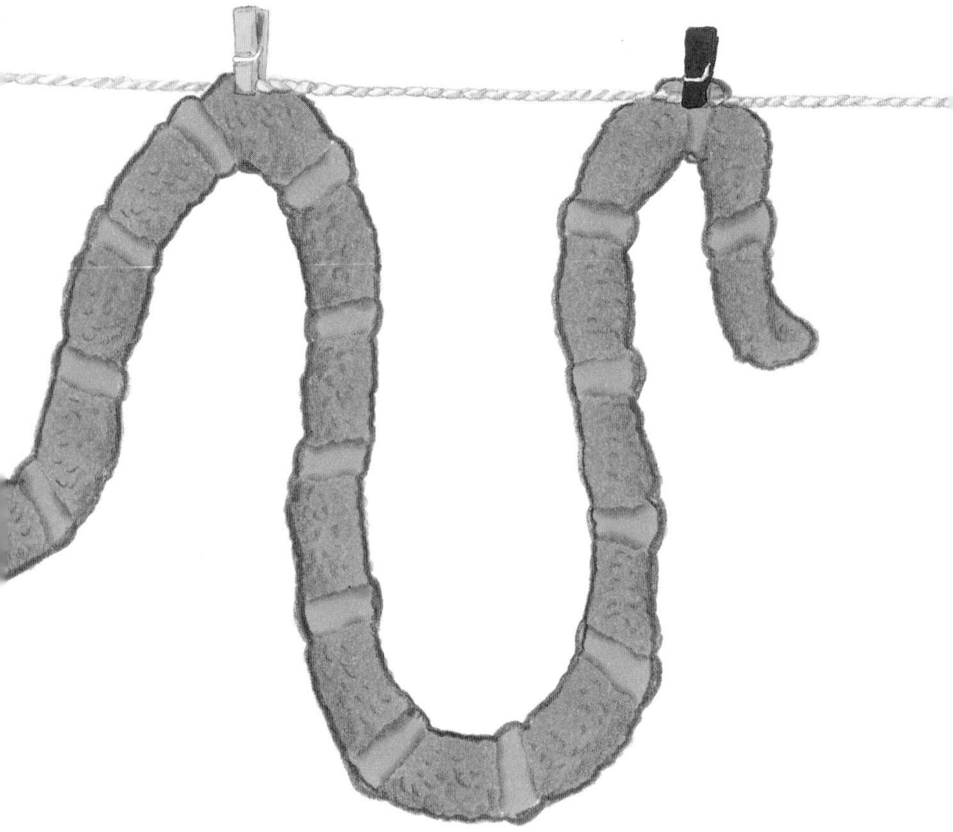

asked the elephant,
the flamingo,
the orang-utan
and the mouse.

What are we going to do now we're all wearing our dry clothes?

asked the flamingo,
the orang-utan,
the mouse
and the giraffe.

said the elephant.

asked the flamingo,
the orang-utan,
the mouse
and the giraffe.

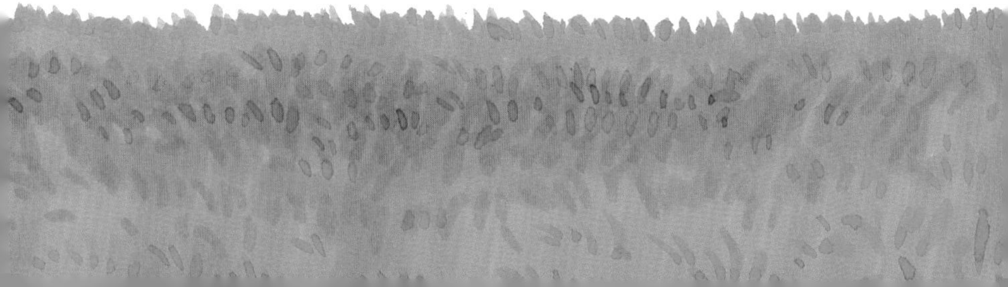

I've got an idea

said the elephant.

LET'S GET THEM WET AGAIN!

WALKER BOOKS is the world's leading independent publisher of children's books. Working with the best authors and illustrators we create books for all ages, from babies to teenagers – books your child will grow up with and always remember. So…

FOR THE BEST CHILDREN'S BOOKS,
LOOK FOR THE BEAR